*For the clan O'Dónncada
but especially for John & Mary*

Humpty Dumpty Rock
a Mother Goose Rap-Along

Produced by David Zaslow
Music by Patti Moran McCoy
Activities by Lawson Inada
Illustrations by Kathleen Bullock
Cover Art by Garrett Miller

Library of Congress Cataloging-in-Publication Data

Mother Goose. Selections.
Humpty Dumpty rock.

(A Mother Goose rap-along)
Summary: A collection of Mother Goose nursery
rhymes grouped together by a common theme. Includes
related activities.
1. Nursery rhymes. 2. Children's poetry.
[1. Nursery rhymes] I. Zaslow, David B., 1947-
II. McCoy, Patti Moran. III. Inada, Lawson Fusao.
IV. Bullock, Kathleen, 1946- ill. V. Title. VI. Series.
PZ8.3.M85 1986g   398'.8   86-21520
ISBN 0-89411-007-1

As I walked by myself and talked to myself,
Myself said unto me,

Word Play

Look to yourself, take care of yourself,
For nobody cares for thee.

I answered myself and said to myself
In the self-same repartee.
Look to yourself, or not yourself
The self-same thing will be.
I would if I could. If I couldn't how could I?
I couldn't unless I could, could I?
Could you unless you could, could you?
I would if I could. If I couldn't how could I?

Three Little Kittens

Three little kittens they lost their mittens
And they began to cry,
Oh, mother dear, we sadly fear
That we have lost our mittens.
What? Lost your mittens, you naughty kittens!
Then you shall have no pie.
Meow, meow, meow. We shall have no pie.
The three little kittens they found their mittens
And they began to cry.
Oh, mother dear, see here, see here,
For we have found our mittens.
Put on your mittens, you silly kittens,
And you shall have some pie.
Purr, purr, purr. Oh, let us have some pie.

The three little kittens put on their mittens
And soon ate up the pie.
Oh, mother dear, we greatly fear
That we have soiled our mittens.
What? Soiled your mittens, you naughty kittens!
Then they began to sigh.
Meow, meow, meow. Then they began to sigh.
The three little kittens they washed their mittens
And hung them out to dry.
Oh, mother dear, do you not hear
That we have washed our mittens?
What? Washed your mittens, then you're good kittens,
But I smell a rat close by.
Meow, meow, meow. We smell a rat close by!

Aiken Drum

There was a man lived in the moon,
And his name was Aiken Drum.
And he played upon a ladle,
And his name was Aiken Drum.
And his hat was made of pizza pies,
And his name was Aiken Drum.
And his coat was made of burger buns,
And his name was Aiken Drum.
And his buttons were made of jelly beans,
And his name was Aiken Drum.
His shoes were made of taco shells,
And his name was Aiken Drum.
His pants were made of leather bags,
And his name was Aiken Drum.

There was a man in another town,
And his name was Willy Wood.
And he played upon a razor,
And his name was Willy Wood.
And he ate up all the pizza pies,
And his name was Willy Wood.
And he ate up all the burger buns,
And his name was Willy Wood.
And he ate up all the jelly beans,
And his name was Willy Wood.
And he ate up all the taco shells,
And his name was Willy Wood.
But he choked upon the leather bags,
And that ended Willy Wood.

Old Mothers

Old Mother Goose, when she wanted to wander,
Would ride through the air on a very fine gander.
She had a house, t'was built in the wood,
Where an owl at the door as sentinel stood.

Old Mother Twitchett has but one eye
And a long tail which she can let fly.
And every time she goes over a gap
She leaves a bit of her tail in a trap.

Old Mother Shuttle lived in a coal-scuttle
Along with her dog and her cat.
What they ate I can't tell but 'tis known very well
That not one of the party was fat.

Old Mother Niddity Nod swore by the pea pod
That she would go to the fair.
Then old Father Peter said he would meet her
Before she got half-way there.

Characters

Georgie Porgie, pudding and pie,
Kissed the girls and made them cry.
When the boys came out to play,
Georgie Porgie ran away.

Wee Willie Winkie runs through the town,
Upstairs and downstairs in his nightgown.
Rapping at the window, crying through the lock,
Are the children all in bed, for now it's eight o'clock?

Jack Sprat could eat no fat.
His wife could eat no lean.
And so between them both, you see,
They licked the platter clean.

Charley Barley, butter and eggs,
Sold his horse for three duck eggs.
When the ducks began to lay,
Charley Barley flew away.

Lucy Locket lost her pocket.
Kitty Fisher found it.
Not a penny was there in it,
Only ribbon round it.

Mary, Mary, quite contrary,
How does your garden grow?
With silver bells and cockle shells
And pretty maids all in a row.

Yankee Doodle came to town
Riding on a pony.
He stuck a feather in his cap
And called it macaroni.

The Queen of Hearts she made some tarts
All on a summer's day.
The Knave of Hearts he stole those tarts
And took them clean away.

Peter, Peter, pumpkin eater,
Had a wife and didn't love her.
Peter learned to read and spell
And then he loved her very well.

Punch and Judy fought for a pie.
Punch gave Judy a knock in the eye.
Says Punch to Judy, will you have any more?
Says Judy to Punch, my eye is too sore!

Humpty Dumpty sat on a wall,
Humpty Dumpty had a great fall.
All the king's horses and all the king's men
Couldn't put Humpty together again.

Humpty
Dumpty

Humpty Dumpty and his brother
Were as like as one another.
Couldn't tell one from the other,
Humpty Dumpty and his brother.

Humpty Dumpty went to town,
Humpty Dumpty tore his gown.
All the needles in the town
Couldn't mend Humpty Dumpty's gown.

Humpty Dumpty sat on a spoon.
Humpty will go in the egg cup soon.
And all the paste and all the glue
Will not make Humpty look like new.

Humpty Dumpty sat on a wall,
Humpty Dumpty had a great fall.
Four score men and four score more
Could not put Humpty where he was before.

Humpty Dumpty sat on a wall,
Humpty Dumpty had a great fall.
All the king's horses and all the king's men
Couldn't put Humpty together again.

Sing A Song Of Sixpence

Sing a song of sixpence,
A pocket full of rye.
Four and twenty blackbirds
Baked in a pie.

When the pie was opened
The birds began to sing.
Was not that a dainty dish
To set before the king?

The queen was in her counting-house
Counting out her money.
The king was in the parlour
Eating bread and honey.

The maid was in the garden
Hanging out the clothes.
There came a little blackbird
Who snapped off her nose.

The Story Of Little Bo-Peep

Once upon a time, there was a young child named Bo-Peep whose special job was to help take care of the newborn lambs. Now, Bo-Peep knew that when lambs are very young they usually have their tails cut off, and in her mind she knew that this protects them from getting sick. But in her heart, it made her feel very sad for the lambs.

Well, one evening Bo-Peep went out to take care of her lambs, but she found that they were gone and her parents hated to hurt Bo-Peep's feelings, so they told her a little fib. They said, "Don't worry. Just leave them alone. They'll come home and they'll still have their tails on."

Happily, Bo-Peep went to sleep and dreamt about her lambs all night. But when she woke up she saw that they were still gone. So she searched in a nearby meadow when suddenly she saw her lambs. But their tails had been cut off! Well, Bo-Peep started to cry, and she even tried to put their tails back on.

Her parents came and told Bo-Peep that they were very sorry for not being really honest with her. And Bo-Peep promised to try, as hard as any kid possibly can, to understand that sometimes there are things that just have to be done, even if they hurt a little at first.

Little Bo-Peep

Little Bo-Peep has lost her sheep
And can't tell where to find them.
Leave them alone and they'll come home
And bring their tails behind them.

Little Bo-Peep fell fast asleep
And dreamt she heard them bleating.
But when she awoke she found it a joke
For they were still all fleeting.

Then up she took her little crook
Determined for to find them.
She found them indeed but it made her heart bleed,
For they'd left their tails behind them.

It happened one day, as Bo-Peep did stray
Into a meadow hard-by.
There she espied their tails side by side
All hung on a tree to dry.

She heaved a sigh and wiped her eye
And over the hillocks went rambling,
And tried what she could, as a shepherdess should,
To tack again each to its lambkin.

Introduction For Parents & Teachers
by David Zaslow & Lawson Inada

Mother Goose rhymes have been loved throughout the world for many generations, and for good reason. The rhymes are fun, entertaining, and easy to learn. They also challenge the imagination in creative ways while providing nuggets of traditional wisdom and learning. Everyone knows and loves Mother Goose! This special Kids Matter edition presents Mother Goose in an entirely new way for today's children: (1) all new music in a variety of contemporary American and multi-ethnic styles; (2) all passages pertaining to sexism, prejudice, and violence have been deleted or revised while retaining the true Mother Goose flavor; (3) many of the four-line rhymes have been combined thematically for the first time to create new, full-length songs and poems; and (4) all the updated lyrics that you hear on the recording are included on these pages for read-along usage.

The section that follows has been carefully developed for children in all age and skill groups. Each of the first eight activity-pages contain three sections. The top section is for preschool and primary age children and contains an illustration with two questions related to a selection in the book. The middle section called *Brain Bender* contains a learning activity for kids who already know how to read and write. The bottom section called *Think About It* is intended for family and classroom discussion. The final pages in the activity section contain a range of creative, entertaining, and challenging activities: Mother Goose trivia facts, poetry writing activities, and a fairly difficult crossword puzzle.

Following are some suggestions for adult participation so that your children and students can get the most out of this unique collection:

Reading: Reading skills can dramatically improve if the rhymes are presented in an exciting and personal way to each child. Parents and teachers should play an active role in both the listening and reading experience. Parents of pre-readers can point to each word as the rhymes are heard. This will create an *association* between the words on the page and the words in the song. Children who can already read can strengthen their skills by being asked to read aloud as the songs are heard. This will reinforce the idea that each song is intended to be read at a different *rate of speed.* Reading ability develops naturally out of excitement and interest. Create an atmosphere of excitement and the skills will follow.

Comprehension: Understanding the content and meanings of the rhymes is based on certain skills that need to be developed. Discuss the ways nonsense, metaphor, and imagination are used to express ideas and feelings. This will strengthen the child's ability to make *inferences* or "educated" guesses. Next, discuss some of the "old fashioned" or difficult words that have been preserved in this edition. Strengthen *dictionary* skills by looking up difficult words or try to figure out the meanings from the *context* in which they are used. Finally, try playing an enjoyable memory game by asking questions about particular songs. For example, "What kind of animal ran up the clock?"

Speaking: Most kids like to perform in a safe and judgement-free setting. Ask your kids to demonstrate their "rapping" skills. They can recite and perform from the book or from memory. Be an encouraging audience and an appreciative listener. Also, participate in the learning process yourself. Dance along, sing along, and even try to make up new rhymes based on the versions in this edition. You'll be setting the right kind of example for your children by demonstrating to them that it's okay to make mistakes while learning. Finally, discuss the diction, accents, and dramatic speaking styles that Steve and Jayne use on the recording.

Appreciation: Music and literary appreciation comes from personal excitement, just like comprehension and reading skills. Encourage your children to participate with the recording by clapping, dancing, and singing along with the various *rhythms.* Try to identify the various instruments and musical *styles* that are heard. Literary appreciation can come from discussions about the history and meanings of the rhymes that are presented by Steve and Jayne before each song. Finally, discuss the revisions and additions that have been made to the rhymes in this Mother Goose collection. Your local library has many collections of traditional children's rhymes and your children will enjoy comparing and talking about the different versions of the same rhymes.

Word Play

Point to the reflection of the lady.

Point to the flower on the lady's hat.

Brain Bender: As you know, people sometimes talk to themselves when they're thinking about things. Imagine that you are taking a walk by yourself and thinking about something. What would you say to yourself? There are no right or wrong answers.

_____

_____

_____

_____

Think About It: What are some of the things you have heard other people saying to themselves?

Three Little Kittens

Count the three kittens.
What is the mother cat leaning on?

Brain Bender: As you know, the *opposite* of <u>lost</u> is <u>found</u>. The *opposite* of <u>cold</u> is <u>hot</u>. Draw a line between the **words** on the *left* and the **opposite words** on the *right*.

Words	Opposite Words
Quiet	Dry
Night	Left
Right	Bottom
Top	Day
Wet	Loud

Think About It: Can you think of something that you lost? Did you find it again?

Aiken Drum

What is on Aiken Drum's head?
What is Willy Wood waiting to do?

Brain Bender: Aiken Drum wears funny clothes made of food. If you could wear some funny *food clothes*, what would you wear? Use your imagination. There are no right or wrong answers.

My hat would be made of _____.

My shirt would be made of _____.

My pants would be made of _____.

My shoes would be made of _____.

Think About It: Of all the people that you know, who can eat the most?

Old Mothers

Point to the three bones.
Point to the fork in the cat's hand.

Brain Bender: As you may know, many *male animals* have their own names. For example, a male goose is called a *gander*. Draw a line between the names of the *animals* and the *male names* of the animals.

Animals	Male Names
Deer	Ram
Duck	Stallion
Elephant	Buck
Horse	Bull
Sheep	Drake

Think About It: Mother Goose lives in a forest. Can you name the closest forest or park to your home?

Characters

Point to the feather in Yankee Doodle's cap.

Are the flowers in the girl's left hand or right hand?

Brain Bender: Listed below are some of the characters from the poem, and some of the things they did. Draw a line between the *characters* and *what they did.*

Characters	What They Did
Lucy Locket	came to town
Punch and Judy	made some tarts
Yankee Doodle	lost her locket
The Queen of Hearts	fought for a pie

Think About It: Can you think of a funny character that you know? What does that person do that is so funny?

Humpty Dumpty

What instrument is Humpty Dumpty playing?
Can you name the different instruments in the picture?

Brain Bender: As you know, some animals are *hatched* from eggs. Chickens are hatched from eggs. Other animals are *born alive* from their mothers. Kittens are born alive from mother cats. Listed below are some animals you know. Circle a "B" if the animal is *born alive,* and circle an "H" if the animal is *hatched* from an egg.

Goose	B	H
Elephant	B	H
Turtle	B	H
Giraffe	B	H
Alligator	B	H

Think About It: What is the name of your favorite musical group? Can you tell why you like the group?

Sing A Song Of Sixpence

Can you find the seven blackbirds in the picture?

What kind of machine is the queen using?

Brain Bender: As you may know, a sixpence is a type of money used in England. Other countries use different types of money. Draw a line between the *countries* and their *types of money*.

Countries	Types of Money
France	Yen
Italy	Peso
Japan	Ruble
Mexico	Lira
Russia	Franc

Think About It: Of all the things you have ever bought, what is your favorite? Can you tell why it is your favorite?

Little Bo-Peep

Point to the two sheep that have ribbons on.

What is thinner, the crook (cane) or the sheep?

Brain Bender: As you know, a group of sheep is called a *flock.* There are different names for different groups of animals. Draw a line between the *animals* and the names of their *groups.*

Animals	Group Names
Geese	School
Bees	Pack
Wolves	Gaggle
Ants	Hive
Fish	Colony

Think About It: Little Bo-Peep is very kind to animals. Can you name some animals that you have helped or been kind to?

A Mother Goose Crossword Pizzazzle

Down Clues

2. A word describing the sounds of sheep (hint: see page 18)
3. A very popular food originally from Italy (hint: see page 6)
5. Another name for "sitting room" (hint: see page 14)
6. What a key fits into (hint: see page 10)
8. Another word for "cane" (hint: see page 18)
10. A shaving instrument (hint: see page 7)
12. What happened to Willie Wood (hint: see page 7)
13. A device for catching animals (hint: see page 8)
14. An article of clothing for the hands (hint: see page 4)
15. A word that means "large dish" (hint: see page 10)
18. A word that means "twenty" (hint: see page 13)
19. A member of the rodent family (hint: see page 5)

Across Clues

1. Another word for "wandering" (hint: see page 19)
4. A large, grassy area (hint: see page 18)
7. A very popular food originally from Mexico (hint: see page 6)
9. Where people gather for entertainment and trade (hint: see page 9)
11. A popular food shaped like little tubes (hint: see page 11)
16. A quick, witty reply (hint: see page 2)
17. A sticky substance useful for mending things (hint: see page 12)
18. Another word for "dirty" (hint: see page 5)
20. Small pies filled with fruit or jam (hint: see page 11)
21. Someone who is a guard (hint: see page 8)
22. A plant used for making flour (hint: see page 14)

Mother Goose Instant Poem

Directions: Create your own "instant poem" by choosing one phrase or word from each of the columns below. Read your instant poem from left to right, then write down your selections in the spaces at the bottom of the page. For example: "Yankee Doodle went in circles riding on a frisbee."

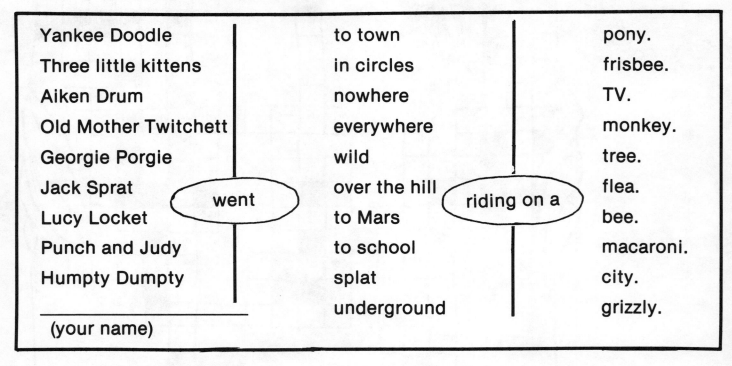

Yankee Doodle		to town	pony.
Three little kittens		in circles	frisbee.
Aiken Drum		nowhere	TV.
Old Mother Twitchett		everywhere	monkey.
Georgie Porgie		wild	tree.
Jack Sprat	_went_	over the hill	_riding on a_ flea.
Lucy Locket		to Mars	bee.
Punch and Judy		to school	macaroni.
Humpty Dumpty		splat	city.
_____ (your name)		underground	grizzly.

Yankee Doodle went _in circles_ riding on a _frisbee_ .

_____ went _____ riding on a _____ .

_____ went _____ riding on a _____ .

_____ went _____ riding on a _____ .

_____ went _____ riding on a _____ .

_____ went _____ riding on a _____ .

_____ went _____ riding on a _____ .

_____ went _____ riding on a _____ .

Mother Goose Trivia Facts

1. Where did the characters of Punch and Judy come from? The characters of Punch and Judy originated in Italy in the sixteenth century.

2. Was Aiken Drum a real person? Aiken Drum is supposed to have been a Scottish soldier in the Battle of Sheriffmuir in 1715.

3. What is Humpty Dumpty called in other countries? In France, "Boule-Boule"; in Sweden, "Thille-Lille"; in Denmark, "Hillerin-Lillerin"; in Switzerland, "Annanadadeli"; in Germany, "Humpelken-Pumpelken."

4. The rhyme about Old Mother Twitchett is a riddle. Can you guess what the rhyme is talking about? What is the answer?

Old Mother Twitchett has but one eye
And a long tail which she can let fly.
And every time she goes over a gap
She leaves a bit of her tail in a trap.

The answer is a needle and thread, and the rhyme describes the act of sewing.

5. What is unusual about the rhyme that goes, "Oh that I were where I would be?" It is the only nursery rhyme included in *The Oxford Book of English Verse.*

6. Where does the rhyme about Yankee Doddle come from? In the American Revolutionary War, it was sung by British troops to make fun of American troops.

Answer Key

Word Play: No right or wrong answer.

Three Little Kittens: quiet/loud, night/day, right/left, top/bottom, wet/dry.

Aiken Drum: There are no right or wrong answers.

Old Mothers: Deer/buck, duck/drake, elephant/bull, horse/stallion, sheep/ram.

Characters: Lucy Locket lost her locket; Punch and Judy fought for a pie; Yankee Doodle came to town; the Queen of Hearts made some tarts.

Humpty Dumpty: Goose/hatched, elephant/born, turtle/hatched, giraffe/born, alligator/hatched.

Sing A Song of Sixpence: France/franc, Italy/lira, Japan/yen, Mexico/peso, Russia/ruble.

Little Bo-Peep: Geese/gaggle, bees/hive, wolves/pack, ants/colony, fish/school.

Music and Project Credits

Project concept: David Zaslow & Lawson Inada

Artwork: Kathleen Bullock, book design & illustrations; Garrett Miller, book and album covers

Composer and Arranger: Patti Moran McCoy

Producer and Writer: David Zaslow

Associate Producer: Patti Moran McCoy

Narrators: Steve Allen and Jayne Meadows

Vocals: Tata Vega on *Word Play* and *Sing A Song of Sixpence;* Lisa Koch on *Characters* and *Humpty Dumpty,* Lisa Koch and David Ashelman on *Little Bo-Peep*

Recording: McCoy Recording Studios, Medford, Oregon; Staunton Studios, Phoenix, Oregon; The Village Recorder, Los Angeles, California

Additional Composing: Jeffrey Bates, composer and arranger of *Characters* and *Humpty Dumpty*

Arrangement and Music Consultant: Jeffrey Bates

Musical Recording Engineer: Jeffrey Bates

Transfer and Effects Engineer: Web Staunton

Voice-Over Engineer: Douglas Williams

Mixdown Engineers: Douglas Williams, Geordie Hormel

Mixdown Assistance: David Zaslow, Patti Moran McCoy, Jeffrey Bates

Production Assistance: Greg Hays

Piano and Keyboards: (Yamaha DX-7, Korg Poly 61) Patti Moran McCoy

Drum Machine Programming: (Yamaha RX-11) Jeffrey Bates

Bass: Alan Trickel

Guitar: Jeffrey Bates

Saxophone: Mike Vannice on *Three Little Kittens*

Children's Chorus: Jodi Campbell, Travis Campbell, Angela Grether, Mandy Grether, Angie Korner, Kelly McCoy, Brittany Miller, Billy Shelton, Liz Shelton, Eva Valdes

Child's Voice and Laughter: Rachel Zaslow

Sound Effects: Alan Trickel, Jeffrey Bates, Michael McCoy, David Zaslow, Douglas Faerber, Patti McCoy, Geordie Hormel, Gregg Vorbeck

Additional Vocals: Linda Morrison on *Three Little Kittens*

Additional Narration: Gregg Vorbeck on *Cats;* Phil Millier and David Zaslow on *Wisdom*

Recommended research sources: The Oxford Dictionary of Nursery Rhymes by Iona and Peter Opie, Oxford University Press; The Annotated Mother Goose by William S. Baring-Gould & Cecil Baring-Gould, Crown Publishers

Very special thanks: Colleen Lewis, children's chorus coordinator; Gena Bates, production aid; Michael Lewis, engineering aid; Milton Gordon, housing and humor; Alphonzo Flores, hospitality; Mary Davis Wilcox & Jack Davis, legal; Jon Trivers, Anne Nicholson, Fred Kier, marketing; Zach Brombacher, John Leffler, manufacturing; Dawn Berry & Arlene McCoy, communications

Our personal thanks: To the partners in The Ed-Ventures Group whose support made this project possible. Loving thanks to Sam Zaslow, Minnie Smith, Derril and Kenneth Kripke; Julia Gordon, Jack & Jean Sargent, Jack Siegel, Debbie Zaslow, & Janet Inada for sharing the dream in the early stages. Finally, our gratitude to Geordie Hormel for his personal encouragement and professional services.